Summer's Over

Eduard Meinema

FLASH & FICTION SERIES

Summer's Over

First published in English: '*Summer's Over*'.

ISBN: 9798662617254
Imprint: Independently published / Copyright by Eduard Meinema, © 2020.

SUMMER'S OVER

A letter? Who still writes letters these days? Anna looked at the envelop as if she discovered an ancient piece of parchment. "Oh my god," she cried out loud for excitement.

It made her father spill coffee on his shirt. "Anna! Really?"

"Sorry dad. But do you know where this letter comes from?"

"The mailman? Just a lucky guess."

"Darryl Simmons! Act like an adult will you?" said Paula Simmons. "And put on a new shirt, baby!"

"I'll finish my coffee first love."

"And how are you going to do that? You've spilled most of it on your shirt."

"Maybe I should squeeze it?" he laughed. Then continued in a different tone: "Now available at your favorite restaurant. Squeezed Spilled Lat Tee."

Paula Simmons didn't respond; she looked at the ceiling instead, seeking for help from higher entities.

"Don't give up on him, mom," said Anna laughing.

"I already did honey. Years ago. He'll never grow up," Paula sighed. "Now show me, what have you got?"

"What? This?" Anna smiled. That's private, mom." She took the envelop and hurried to her room. Her hands were shaking when she opened the envelop. This was exciting. Even more thrilling than opening an email. Carefully she unfolded the paper only to find the letter was no more than a note with a few mysterious words: 'Found you before you were lost'. She turned the sheet of paper around. *"That's all? No name, no address; nothing but a riddle? Not even a clue about the sender?"* The knocking on the door stopped her from worrying. "Who's there?"

"It's me. Dad."

Anna smiled. "No need to add 'dad'; I can tell by the darkness of your voice."

With the lowest tone his vocal cords could produce, he said: "Oh, alright dear. It's me, a voice out of the gloom".
She opened the door. "Come in silly."

"Good news?"

"Don't know dad. It's some kind of riddle, I just don't understand it."

"I see… Maybe this will help?" said Darryl while laying a package on Anna's bed.

"What's that?"

"Don't ask me, just open it up. It's a special delivery, all for you. It came in together with the letter."

"Why didn't you tell me right away?" She sounded offended, but her curiosity won. She ripped off the bubble paper and hastily opened the box. "No way!"

she shouted.

"No?" said Darryl surprised and curious.

"Jimmy Choo!"

"No way!" Darryl shouted imitating his daughter's voice with sarcasm. "…Have I met this guy?"

"Dad… They are shoes!"

"Oh sorry, I thought you said Choo."

"Bless you."

"What?"

"Just one of those stupid jokes you always make dad."

Then they both started to laugh.

"What's so funny?" Paula asked.

"Inside joke, mom. Hey! Have a look at this mom. Real Jimmy Choo shoes!"

"Wow that is… wow…"

"Glad you've cleared that out," said Darryl smiling. "Now, am I the only one not understanding the precious value of this gift?"

"This is a girl's thing honey. Don't interfere," said Paula gently touching the shoes.

"Never heard you about this choo-choo guy before," Darryl complained.

"That's because you cannot afford to buy me shoes like this love."

"I can't?" he said suddenly concerned about his financial status.

"Read this mom," said Anna; she handed the note to her mother.

Paula read it out loud: "*Found you before you were lost*? Some mysterious guy to send you such a note."

"Let me see," said Darryl.

"See what?" Anna asked.

"The note and the envelop. There must be some kind of address upon it."

"I have checked it dad, nothing there. Not a clue." Darryl studied the labels thoroughly. "Peculiar. I thought mail delivery services never accepted packages without knowing the sender."

"There's a code printed above our address. Why don't you call the parcel service and ask them to trace the sender by the code?" said Paula.

"Good thinking. Will do," said Darryl.

"You think they are not meant for me?" Anna asked disappointed.

Paula took her daughter in her arms. "We're just careful Anna. We don't want anyone to hurt you."

"I hoped it was from… you know. Jaime?"

Paula gave her daughter a faint smile. "He was a nice boy Anna; but no more than a summer love."

Anna's face shivered. She was nearly crying.

"Oh Anna. I told you before; you should get him out of your head."

Her lips started to tremble. "I can't," she said.

"Anyway, he doesn't know your address, does he?"

"I wish he did."

"Don't count on it dear. Like I said. Forget about him."

"Who else will send me these expensive shoes?"

"Dad is making a call right now Anna. Let's wait and hear what he finds."

Waiting for Darryl to finish his phone call, Anna tried the new shoes. Then she studied the note again. Nothing specific about it. A regular sheet of paper, the ink of the letters seemed to have run out; the text probably printed with some kind of inkjet printer. "Maybe it's some kind of reverse Cinderella story. He sends me shoes that fit me perfect; hoping I will wear them to a party where I will lose one. As he already knows where I live, he immediately knows where to find me."

"Sure, and you live happily ever after. Sweet dreams girl."

"You have no imagination mom."

"Oh, but I do. I imagine someone may hurt you."

"That's pessimism; negativity which has nothing to do with imagination."

"I'm just careful Anna."

"Why?" said Anna not understanding her mother's concern.

"Because there's every reason to in this world," Darryl interrupted. "Your mother is right Anna. You cannot trust anyone anymore. It's a crazy world."

"Both of you are too concerned," she complained.

"What did you find Darryl?" Paula was curious to know. "Did they know who the sender is?"

"No. But they assured me they usually do not deliver packages if the sender is unknown."

"Thanks, that makes me feel much more comfortable. And now what?"

"Yes dad, now what?"

Darryl hesitated. "Well, returning them seems to be impossible. So you might as well enjoy your gift." He looked at his daughter. "But I can tell you already do."

Anna stared at the shoes she was wearing. "Real Jimmy Choo," she sighed. *And I hope they do come from him,* she said to herself. For a moment she felt the glorious heartbeating from last summer again; remembering the joyful days they had spend together.

Anna peeked through the window. Hoping; no praying, he would be standing there. Of course he wasn't. He lived at the other side of the country. All the way at the West coast.

Downstairs Darryl sat down next to his wife. "Strange isn't it" he said.
"What is dear?"
"That parcel services claim not to deliver any packages without a sender, but yet we have one right here."
"Hmm, yes, peculiar," said Paula, her fingers swiping on her tablet.
"You know what I find most strange?"
"What's that?" she answered without really knowing what she was responding to.
"The addressee."
"Is it?"
"You're not really listening are you?"
Paula looked up from her tablet. "What love?"
Darryl only stared at her.
"Sorry," she apologized. "I was checking some of our vacation photos."
Darryl peeked upon her tablet. "I can tell. But like I said, what I find strange is the addressee of the package." He paused; waited for Paula to react. When she didn't, he continued: "There was no label upon the package Paula, so when the delivery boy handed me the package and the letter, I assumed they were meant for Anna. But when I called the delivery service, they told me the package was meant for you Paula."
She looked up in surprise. "What? You mean those shoes were actually meant for me?"

"Unbelievable. Is that all you can think off?" said Darryl irritated.

"Why are you so upset?"

"Cause we've received an expensive gift from mister Nobody which I gave to Anna who now thinks mister Summer love has send her a secret message, while in fact it was meant for you, send by mister Do You Remember Me."

"Oh sweetie, you're jealous."

"I'm not…" Darryl pounded his fist on the couch. He bit on his lip. "We both know perfectly well what happened there last summer Paula," he said restrained. He refused to look her in the eyes.

Paula didn't say a word. She looked out of the window. Ashamed. "I…"

"Don't!" he said gruffly.

"We need to talk it over Darryl," Paula tried.

"I don't want to," he grumbled.

"But honey…"

Darryl stood up. "Don't patronize me Paula. I'm not stupid," he said before he walked out of the room.

Paula remained seated; trying to fight the tears. When she was sure Darryl could not see her anymore, she released her watery eyes.

*

"Honey, will you answer the door?" Paula Simmons was enjoying her morning shower. She carefully listened if Darryl bothered to answer. He hadn't said anything since last night.

The repetitive sound of the doorbell started to annoy her. Dressed in a towel, to cover up her nakedness, she walked to the front door. Her bare, wet feet left a watery track upon the floor.

"Fuck!" she said when she opened the door.

"Well, hello to you too,' said Jaime, gazing at the half naked woman in front of him. "Were you expecting me?"

"Get the fuck out of here!" she replied with anger.

"Wow, that's a lot of fucking this early in the morning," Jaime smiled.

"Who is it?" Darryl suddenly asked, standing right behind Paula.

Quickly she closed the door. "Jesus Darryl, do really need to sneak up on me? You scared the shit out of me."

"That's not a pretty thought."

"Darryl! Stop kidding."

He paused for a short while; then repeated: "Well. Who is it?"

"No one… Someone… I told him to leave."

"I can hear he's still standing there," said Darryl. He pushed his wife aside, reopened the door and stared into the smiling face of Jaime. "Fuck!" he said, badly surprised.

"You all call me that name? My mother calls me Jaime, you know…"

"I don't know your mother…"

"Really?"

"…and I don't really care to know her."

"Don't say things you might regret," said Jaime confident.

"Get the fuck out of my house," Darryl yelled. "Get out of my town; get out of my life." He didn't wait for Jaime to respond, but immediately slammed the door and turned to his wife. "That says it all, right?"

"What do you mean?" said Paula, now shivering in the hall.

"Yesterday's package? It was his. Damned." He pounded his fist into the wall.

"Yeah, alright Darryl. You've said that before. No need to get mad."

"No? Don't I? I thought we both agreed Anna would not see this guy. Or is there another reason for him to pop up at our door? Do *you* want to see him? That's it, right? He actually came to see you. Well?"

"I'm not having that conversation right now," said Paula. "I'll finish showering first."

"It's never the right time. Is it Paula?" said Darryl while his wife returned to the bathroom. "Yeah okay. You run girl. Hide away, don't bother my feelings."

"Act like a man Darryl," was all he heard before Paula slammed the door. A few seconds later he heard the water running.

*

"Did you come to your senses Darryl?" said Paula, bringing him another coffee in the study.

Darryl sighed. "I just don't like it," he said. "This guy has ruined our vacation and now he's back."

"Ruined, ruined," Paula shook her head. "Anna had the time of her life."

"I'll bet she did… until she finds out what you've been doing." He looked at his wife inquisitively.

Paula sat down upon his desk. "I told you before Darryl, it didn't mean anything."

"If so, why did you do it? And why is he coming

here?"

"Darryl it was a one night stand! I've made a mistake and I'm sorry about it, alright? I didn't even know he was seeing our daughter at the time."

"Oh, so then it is okay? No big deal? What if I had betrayed you Paula? How would you feel?"

"We didn't exactly have a thrilling sex life at the time..." she excused herself.

Her attitude made him desperate. "Look.. I'm willing to forgive you, to forget about what happened. But I don't know what I'll do to him if he's coming back into our life. And mind you, he is persuasive!"

Paula bit upon her lip. "Honestly Darryl... I don't want to lose you. And I can't tell whether he came all the way to meet Anna or..., you know..."

"To see you again," said Darryl down. "We both know the answer Paula. Anna only was, and is, just an excuse for him to see you. Just like he did last summer."

Paula looked down to the floor. "Sorry," she sighed.

Darryl stood up. Put his arms around his wife. "We've got to get rid of him Paula. He will be stalking us... Anna... He will ruin our life."

"Maybe he won't come back."

Darryl looked her into the eyes. "You know he will honey. You know."

She sniveled. "Promise me you won't tell Anna."

Gently he caressed her hair. "Promised you before love. She doesn't have to know."

*

"I'm home!" Anna threw her bag upon the small

table in the hallway.

"Hi dear, how was your day?" said Paula.

"Mom, you won't believe it… he was there!" Anna shouted excited.

Paula was startled. "Who was?" she asked fearing what Anna was going to tell her.

"Jaime," she smiled. "He was waiting for me at college!"

Paula's lips started to tremble.

"Isn't it exciting mom?" Anna danced around. "And you know what? He's coming over tonight!"

"That's… that's, nice…" Paula quivered. "Does your father know?"

"Of course not silly. I'm telling you first. Why? What is it? You don't seem to be happy."

Paula didn't know how to react. "No. No, there's nothing," she hesitated. She knew she had to tell Darryl before Anna would. "Why don't you get a drink and a sandwich love? I'll go and find dad."

"You don't mind do you?" said Anna, her innocent blue eyes followed the insecure moves of her mother.

"I… well, … Let me find dad sweetie.' With shaky hands Paula placed a soda upon the table. "I'll be right back," she said before she left Anna wondering behind.

A few minutes later Paula hurried back, trying to keep up with Darryl. A few steps ahead of her, he rushed into the room eager to hear the news from Anna herself. "Anna? Is it true?"

"Yeah dad, isn't it great?" Anna laughed.

Darryl sat down on the leather couch, next to his daughter. "I am… thrilled." He execrated the brat, but he didn't have the guts to tell the truth to his only daughter.

Hooked by the promise he had made to his wife. The truth about Jaime would be kept secret.

Sitting so close to her dad, she could almost feel something was wrong. "Your face seems to be telling something else…"

Darryl tried to pretend he didn't hear what she just said. "So, he came to look for you at college?" he said compulsively cheerful.

"Yes. Oh dad it was such a surprise." Over excited she started to tell everything at once: "I was walking there with my friends, you know, Joanie and Hanna, the one with the red curly hair, I mean Hanna, Joanie has black hair, again, guess she was bored with being blond or so, anyway, all of a sudden someone called my name; and I didn't recognize his voice at first, but then he called me again, and I saw him standing there, dad, he was waiting there, for me!"

The words cascaded into Darryl's head. "Slow down, will you? You make me feel dizzy."

"Sorry dad, but, don't you get it? He was there. I was so excited!"

"Seems to me you still are love."

"I am, I am! And he's coming over tonight. If you don't mind of course. Ooh, I can't wait for him to be here."

Darryl's mind was working top speed. He had to find a way out. This guy was unwanted; not allowed to return. Darryl didn't want him to come back into their lives. He had to find a way out. He had to convince Anna she shouldn't be seeing him.

"Do you dad? Do you?"

"What love?"

"Do you mind he's coming over tonight?"

Darryl looked up to Paula. Her eyes almost panicked. "You know Anna… I think it would be wise…"

Anna stood up, stamped her feet upon the floor, almost cracking the heels of her expensive designer shoes. "Come on dad, I am seventeen, you cannot decide what's good or bad for me. Other girls my age are travelling the world all by themselves!" she shouted.

"Lower you voice Anna! Those girls have irresponsible parents."

"Oooh dad, you are so old fashioned."

"Well, that's about the first time you admit I do know something about fashion."

"Those stupid jokes are only making it worse. Now I don't care if you don't want Jaime to come over. I'll be going out with him. And there's no way you can stop me." Anna ran to her bedroom.

"Well done," said Paula disappointed.

Darryl shrugged his shoulders. "What did you want me to do?"

"You may not like the idea," said Paula carefully, "but I think we should invite Jaime over here. I don't want those kids to go out by themselves."

"How?" said Darryl whispering; his teeth tightly upon each other. "How do you think I feel when I see that dirty little brat again? The guy who…" he tried to temper his voice even more, so Anna would not hear a thing he said. Agitated he continued: "The guy who fucked my wife? You really think I will tolerate him in my own house?"

Paula sat down on her knees; laying both of her hands upon Darryl's legs. With tears in her voice, she said: "Honey, you know I am sorry. And I really, really don't want to see him. But you know as well as I do, that boy is persistent. He is determined to get back to… tome, I guess. If we don't accept him, don't invite him in to our house, he will use Anna to get to me. He will follow her anywhere without either one of us knowing. We will have to live with the fear he will seduce her, or maybe hurt her, every single day. Until he finally will be with me again."

"I should go to the police."

"To do what Darryl? Tell them your wife enjoyed a toy-boy during the vacation? You will certainly make their day. Why should they stop him? He hasn't done anything yet. No. The only way to get him out of our life is to fight him."

"Fight him? How… What do you mean…? You're telling me I have to kill him?" Darryl stammered.

"Offense is the best defense?"

"But Anna…"

"Forget what we have promised ourselves, honey. If we don't fight him, he will be stalking us forever. Imagine the bad things he may do to Anna. I know she will be mad, but it's for the better. She will understand. Eventually."

Biting his nails, Darryl said: "Alright…alright, tell Anna to invite him. Let's fight! Let's get it over with."

Paula kissed him on his forehead. "The sooner the better love."

*

Anna hopped into the hall the moment she heard the door bell. Glad to finally meet her summer love again. Paula and Darryl remained seated; nervous, almost frozen.

"He's here!" Anna giggled, hanging on Jaime's arm.

Jaime said hello with an underhand grin upon his face which made Darryl instantly go insane.

"Hello Jaime. Nice to… see you again," said Paula hesitating. She pinched Darryl's arm, in a desperate attempt to control both of their feelings. Which succeeded; at least for the moment.

With a somewhat scary low voice Darryl only mumbled "Jaime".

"Well, let's be seated," said Paula kind of cheerful.

"Oh, I have brought you something mrs. Simmons," said Jaime. He gave her a bottle of perfume. He had to come close to her to present his little gift, giving him the opportunity to whisper seductively into her ear: "I know what you like."

"Thank you," said Paula; her cheeks all red. "Let's have dinner. Anna, you and Jaime sit over there, Darryl and I will sit on the other side." Quickly she ran off to the kitchen.

"Need a hand Paula?" The moment he said it, Darryl realized whatever he was going to say would have to be more convincing. Leaving Jaime no doubt about his feelings. "Can I help you love?"

"Yes please, sweetie," Paula answered.

When he stepped into the kitchen, he found Paula bended over the worktop. "Hang on love," he whispered. "We're in this together."

"I think we'd better leave all of the knifes in the kitchen," she replied, making them both laugh.

"That's the spirit," said Darryl. "So, in which glass did you put the poison?"

She kissed him on his lips. "Oh Darryl, I wish summer was over."

"I wish this evening was," said Darryl impatient. "Ready?"

Paula took the plates in her hands. "Ready," she confirmed.

"I wasn't sure what you like," said Paula when she handed Jaime a plate. "So I made pasta. Everybody likes pasta, right?"

"Smells delicious Paula… Do you mind if I call you Paula?" He took the plate out of her hands, softly touching her arm.

"No, I mean, I don't mind," she said hastily withdrawing her hands.

"Bon appétit," said Darryl. "Enjoy!"

"I already do," said Jaime.
Darryl closed his eyes, trying to ignore his anger. "So, Jaime that must have been quite a journey, from the West coast all the way here to the East coast."

"Planes travel quick mister Simmons," said Jaime; knowingly not calling Darryl by his first name.
Anna giggled. Holding Jaime's hand underneath the table she was having the best time of her life.

"And what made you decide to come all this way?"

"I'm not sure what you mean mister Simmons", said Jaime provocative.

Anna looked estranged at her father. *What was he up to?*

Paula quickly intervened, saying: "He means if you are you here for a holiday? Or visiting family?"

"Oh, I see Paula. No I'm here for you."

Startled Paula dropped her glass of wine. While she tried to wipe the wine from her dress, she said: "Excuse me?"

"I came to see you all," Jaime grinned. "But most of all Anna, of course." Thoughtful he turned to Anna and kissed her on the cheek. "I think I will hang around."

The girl reacted delighted. "You will? You're going to stay?"

"He needs a job first Anna," said Darryl pragmatic.

"I think he needs a place to stay first dad. We have a spare room, why can't he stay there?"

Before her parents could react, Jaime said: "Oh, Paula, that would be nice, wouldn't it?"

"Are you out of your mind?" Darryl growled. "He cannot stay here."

"Why not dad? We're not even using that room."

"Yes '*dad*'? Why not?" Jaime laughed. "I'm a perfect guest. I will not enter Anna's bedroom without your permission. Or yours, but that's up to Paula of course…"

"You…" Darryl jumped from his seat, ready to cross the table.

Paula could barely stop him. "Calm down, Darryl. Don't get upset."

"Dad! Take it easy will you? He only said he will not enter any room without your permission. Out of respect. I think that's pretty neat. Why are you acting so strange tonight?"

"Cause… arrgh," Darryl madly stamped his feet. "Cause you don't know him Anna. You don't know who Jaime really is, or what he has done. That's why."

Anna looked at her angry father. There was a man she had never seen before. "Dad, we all know Jaime; he spend almost the entire summer with us. Why are you doing this? Why are you ruining this evening?"

"Yes, mister Simmons, why are you?" said Jaime defiant.

Darryl was shaking all over. Even though Paula had managed to keep him at her side of the table for now, she knew she could not hold him much longer.

"He's a betrayer," Darryl shouted out of control. "He deceives you. And me!"

"No Darryl, don't!" Paula shouted, vainly trying to keep her man from jumping across the table.

Jaime quickly stood up. "Wow, keep it easy mister Simmons. I don't know what you are talking about."

"Dad! Knock it off! Don't hurt him", Anna yelled at the madman now standing on the table.

Darryl snorted like a caveman. "Get the hell out of my house! Get out or I will throw you out!"

"But mister Simmons, why? We have so much in common…"

Outrageous Darryl jumped from the table. In a flash, Jaime grabbed Anna from her chair and used her as a human shield. "You're not going to hurt your little girl now, are you?"

Both Simmons girls were shouting and crying out loud.

"Anna! Get out of the way!" Darryl commanded.

"I'm not letting her go, mister Simmons, not until you have calmed down."
Paula pulled Darryl by his arms. "Calm down, Darryl. Stop it!"
Darryl put his hands up high. "Alright, alright, I'm calm. I won't hurt you Jaime; but you have to leave. You and I understand each other, right?"

Jaime acted innocent. "Not really, mister Simmons, I came to visit your… girl. That's all."

"Which one of my girls, you filthy rat?"
Anna didn't know where to look anymore. What were they talking about? "Mom?" she softly cried. "Can you please tell me what this is all about?"
Paula stood in tears. The make-up she had been working on all afternoon had now flown all over her face. She blamed herself for this dreadful evening; she could have seen this coming.

"Mom?" Anna sniffed desperate. "Jaime?" she asked, looking up at the man behind her. Neither one of them answered. Then she looked at the mad man in front of her. "Dad? Can you explain me what this is all about? Please?"

"That pervert slept with your mom," Darryl spoke loud and avowedly.
There.
It had been said.
Jaime didn't resist when Anna outwrestled herself from his arms.
She was gasping. "Mom? You… and…? Why?" she cried.

"Oh, it didn't mean anything Anna. That's what she told me. Just a mistake, that's all."
Agitated Paula looked at him. "Thought we were in this together?" she said irritated.
Anna turned to Jaime, hitting her hands upon his chest. "Why Jaime, why? Because I didn't want to go to bed with you?"
Darryl became even madder, hearing his daughter in pain.

"And why did you come all the way? Were you

hoping to get laid again?" Anna continued.

Paula was shaking her head. "I didn't want this. Honestly. I just… It was all a mistake", she sighed.

"No Paula, it wasn't a mistake. You knew perfectly well what you were doing that night. It was pure lust, and you liked it," said Darryl angry.

"Did she mister Simmons?" said Jaime. "Are you sure she knew what she was doing? You're damned sure it was a mistake?"

"It takes two to tango boy. You wanted to have sex with my wife; she wanted you just as bad. No doubt about it."

"And how can you be so sure about that mister Simmons? Have you been in such a situation before?"

"Paula knows I've always been faithful to her."

"And to your brother too I guess?"

"My brother? What has John got to do with this? I haven't seen him for years."

Paula and Anna were standing in between the two quarreling men. Flabbergasted. "Somehow, I feel this is not about me anymore," said Paula.

"Somehow, I don't understand anything at all anymore," said Anna. "And I wonder if any of these two men knows…"

The men were facing each other like two opponents who just stepped into the ring. Waiting for the first one to have the guts to do something.

"And what has uncle John got to do with this; huh? Jaime?" said Anna. "It's true; we haven't seen him for years."

"I know," said Jaime. "Did you ever wonder why you haven't seen him? Or your aunt?"

"Aunt Vicky?" said Anna surprised. "Aunt Vicky

and uncle John separated long before I was born."

"Right… how long ago exactly? Any idea?"

"Like I said, I wasn't even born. I'm seventeen… must have been twenty years or more."

"Twenty years or more… I'm twenty-one," said Jaime.

"Where is this going to?" said Paula staring unbelieving at Darryl, the man she thought she had known so well for all these years.

"Will you tell her mister Simmons? Or should I do it, *dad*?" said Jaime with another grin upon his face.

Anna scared up: "Dad? You're calling my dad… *dad*?"

"Darryl?" said Paula restless.

"Dad?" said Anna confused.

Darryl was just standing there, his mouth wide open; as if he had been beaten by a truck. Not knowing what to say, he stuttered: "I… I… How? What? When? I didn't know."

"Didn't know what Darryl? Tell me," Paula demanded.

"Never noticed the way he fancied aunt Vicky, Paula?" said Jaime. "And never questioned yourself why Darryl visited her so often, especially when his brother was on another assignment for the army? Nah, you didn't. You're too good to be true Paula. You really are. But Darryl isn't. He slept with Vicky until the day John found out. But then it was too late, wasn't it, *dad*? John didn't find out until the day I was born. Until the doctors at the hospital told John, his son had a rare blood type, he didn't have himself. But he knew you have…"

They all gazed at each other. Slowly realizing all

relations had just been rearranged forever.

"So, you are Darryl's… son?" Paula finally broke the silence.

"I am…auntie."
Paula shivered. Why oh why did she sleep with him?

"What… what happened to aunt Vicky?" said Anna with a trembling voice.

"That's the most painful part. John told her to leave."

"And how about you?" Paula asked.

"Vicky had to take me with her. We travelled around like gypsies. From one town to another. Didn't receive any support from John, or my father… Until Vicky realized she was hunted."

"Hunted?" said Paula surprised.

"Vicky decided to bring me to a shelter. A safe place where I could grow up without being found. I have never heard of my mother again; never been able to find her. Till one day I was watching a TV-series about unsolved crimes. I recognized my mother instantly. I only have one picture of my mom, but it definitely was her. Murdered. I decided to find the murderer before he would hurt anyone else. It didn't took me long to find the three of you. But I had to be careful. I was afraid he might hurt you if he would find out who I really am. He killed my mom; no need to victimize more people. Right, *dad*?"

"You mean… Darryl…?" said Paula anxious and completely overwhelmed.

"Yes Paula. Your husband is a cold blooded adulterous murderer, sleeping with several women. And believe me; he would have killed you just as easy as he did my mom. But I found you just in time."

"Found you before you were lost," said Anna.
Jaime smiled. "You've got it Anna."
The three of them looked down on the pathetic man sitting on the floor. "You still expect me to leave, *dad*?" said Jaime.
Darryl looked at his wife. Ashamed. But not saying anything.

"I think it's perfectly clear who's leaving this house," said Paula. "Anna, Jaime; let's eat. Mister Simmons will not join us. He is going to pack his things."

"You mean you let him get away with murder?" said Anna not understanding. "You allow him to go and spend the rest of his life with another woman? Or one of many women he sleeps with?"

"No. He's going to pack up all his things and then he's going to report himself. Or I will," said Paula. She sat down at the dinner table, her dress all messed up from the red wine she had spilled, and started to eat. When she looked out of the window, she saw the leaves falling from the trees.

Autumn, she thought.
Finally.

ABOUT THE AUTHOR

Did you enjoy reading this story? Then read some more! Check out my website www.eduardmeinema.nl for all my compelling stories and artwork.

Newsletter

Sign up to my fiveweekly newsletter; be the first to hear about new releases, get yourself a discount and, for starters, receive a free ebook! Visit my website www.eduardmeinema.nl for registering.